The Adventures of ARNIE the DOUGHNUT

INVASION of the UFONUTS

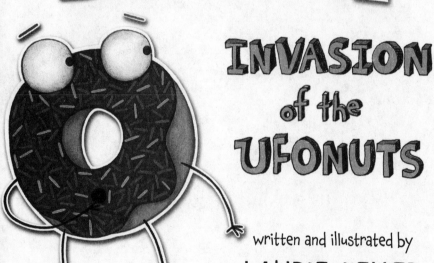

written and illustrated by

LAURIE KELLER

SQUARE FISH

Christy Ottaviano Books

Henry Holt and Company — New York

The **WHOLE TIME** I thought it was the meatball who did it, but it turned out to be that sweet little french fry. It was the scariest movie I've **EVER** seen. I have to give it my highest rating—

5 out of **5** sprinkles!

ARNie and PeeZo at the MOVIES

I didn't like it one bit. It wasn't even scary.

WHAT?!

Was the director SLEEPING when he made this film? He completely ruined the scene where the meatball and the french fry come face-to-face. Any good director knows that a little dramatic lighting and some high/low camera angles make things WAY scarier. I'm giving it my lowest rating—

0 out of **5** pizza toppings!

ya see, that's one of the things
I like best about being friends
with Peezo—we don't always
agree on everything but we
STILL get along.

Hey, a bunch of news trucks are in the parking lot. I bet **Queenie LaTaffy** is being interviewed again. Queenie LaTaffy is the latest teen tuba-playing sensation, and she passed through town last week to visit her aunt Chewy.

Peezo **LOVES** her and wants to get her autograph more than *anything*. Her new song, *OOMPAH-OOMPAH WOW-WOW*, has been **#1** on the *TOP 40 TUBA HITS* chart for three weeks in a row!

Peezo, I think Queenie LaTaffy is outside.

Queenie LaTaffy!

Queenie LaTaffy!

Queenie LaTaffy!

The newspeople aren't interviewing Queenie LaTaffy or ANY famous person—they're interviewing my neighbor, Loretta Schmoretta! I wonder what's going on.

Folks, it looks like we've got a real outer space—or in THIS case, outer SPASTRY—story on our hands. Loretta Schmoretta is the sixteenth person today claiming to have been abducted by alien doughnuts, then released after the aliens stole their Downtown Bakery doughnuts! Tell us more, Loretta.

Okay.

Well, I was walking through the parking lot to my apartment with my bag of **DOWNTOWN BAKERY** doughnuts when I heard a **LOUD CLINKING** noise overhead. I looked up and saw a **FLYING SAUCER** floating above me! Actually, it was a flying **CUP** and saucer. I tried to run but a glowing beam of green, sticky jelly stopped me in my tracks. **SUDDENLY I** was inside the spacecraft, surrounded by gigantic **DOUGHNUT CREATURES!** There must have been a **DOZEN** of them!

They kept staring at me and mumbling to one another. I couldn't understand a word they said. They just stared and mumbled.

STARED AND MUMBLED.

STARED AND MUMBLED.

STARED AND MUMBLED

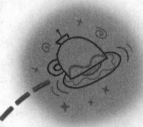

Yeah, we get it. THEN what happened?

Then they grabbed my doughnuts, and next thing I knew I was back on the ground. I saw them fly off and I haven't seen them since!

What's going on out here? Are you two okay?

Loretta Schmoretta just told reporters that she was abducted by alien doughnuts from outer spastry, and they're planning to take over Earth, Mr. Bing!

Oh, BROTHER!
What will she think of NEXT?!

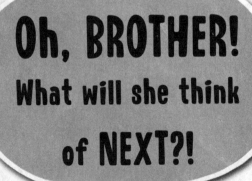

I had a feeling Mr. Bing wouldn't believe her. He says Loretta Schmoretta is **ALWAYS** making up stories. **LAST YEAR** she told reporters that

GEORGE WASHINGTON

stopped by, begging for a piece of the **CHERRY PIE** she'd just made for her grandson's school carnival.

It was DELICIOUS—I ate three pieces!

I suppose she **DOES** come up with some rather unusual stories. I mean, *REALLY*—the idea of alien doughnuts wanting to take over Earth? That's pretty far-fetched! But why did all those OTHER people say they saw them, too?

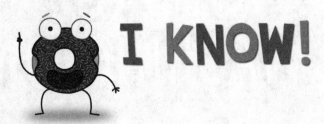

I KNOW!

Maybe Mr. Baker Man put too much **SUGAR** in the doughnut batter, and it made people see strange things—like alien doughnuts from outer spastry.

Get away from me, you scary alien doughnut!

Knock it off, Gerald.

Or maybe it was one of those hidden camera shows that plays jokes on people, and they had a team of actors dressed up like alien doughnuts. **I LOVE THOSE SHOWS!**

Take me to your knead-er!

Well, *WHATEVER* it was, I'm sure people have forgotten *ALL* about it by now.

19

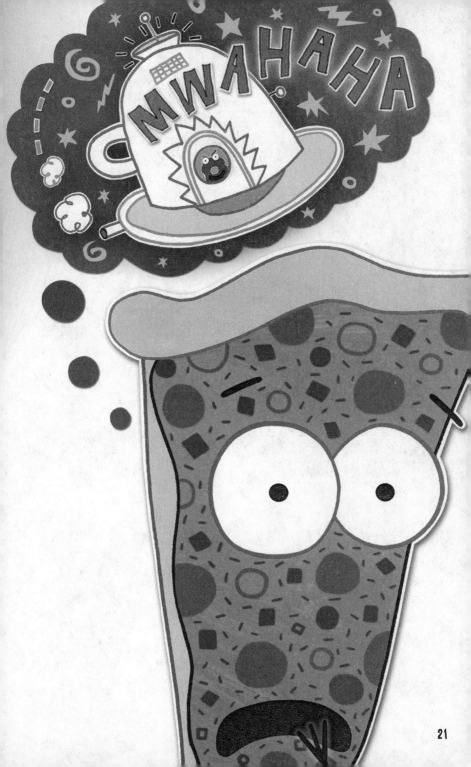

21

I *said*, I can't believe that man thought I was an alien doughnut. Can *YOU*, Peezo?

Uhhh...no. Ummm. I don't know.

What do you mean, *you don't know?*

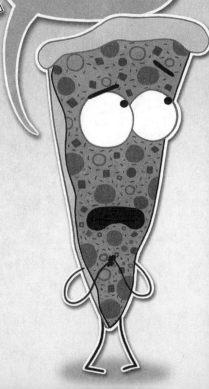

Well, you **ARE** pretty strange, now that I think about it, Arnie. I mean, I was made to be eaten, and if someone ever decides to eat me, I won't mind. YOU were made to be eaten, too, but when Mr. Bing tried to eat you, you **FLIPPED OUT!** And look at you now— you're his DOUGHNUT-DOG!

That doesn't make me an *alien*, Peezo.
Well, what about your *name*?
My *name*?

All the letters in **ARNIE** and **ALIEN** are the same except for one. You changed the **L** in **ALIEN** to an **R** and then mixed up the letters to spell **ARNIE**. I can't believe I didn't see it sooner—

YOU'RE an ALIEN DOUGHNUT from OUTER SPASTRY!

(Le French Cruller)

OH, THAT PEEZO MAKES ME SO MAD!

Some friend *HE* is, accusing me of being an ALIEN DOUGHNUT FROM OUTER SPASTRY! And after all the times I've stuck up for him. Why, just yesterday a mean bunch of overripe bananas started picking on him . . .

. . . and I GROWLED at them until they ran off.

And **THIS** is how he repays me?! OKAY, I probably shouldn't have told that hungry lady to eat him. But I couldn't help it—

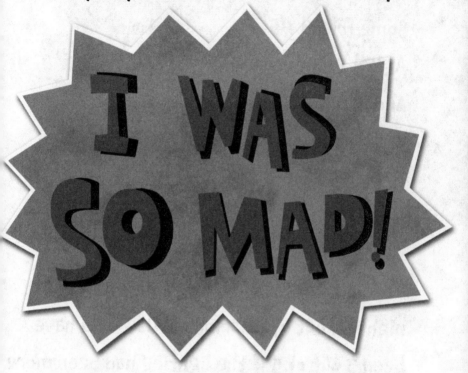

Besides, as much as he CLAIMS he doesn't mind being eaten, I know he'd never **REALLY** let anyone do that!

CHAPTER 4

My friend is an alien doughnut from OUTER SPASTRY!

AHHH!

I had a **REALLY SCARY** nightmare last night—4 out of 5 sprinkles! (It would have been 5 out of 5 if the lighting had been more dramatic.) Peezo accused me of being an alien doughnut from outer spastry, I told a hungry lady she should eat him for lunch, and a Ninja Waffle tried to steal my sprinkles. It all seemed SO REAL!

It **WAS** real! Well, everything except the part about ME. I saw you were having a nightmare and it looked like fun, so I joined in. Sorry I scared you. I **WOULD** like some of those sprinkles, though. Got any extra?

YES, it's all coming back to me now. That was the first argument Peezo and I have **EVER HAD.**

UGGGHHH, my stomach hurts.

COME ON, ARNIE—IT'S TIME FOR OUR WALK!

What's wrong, Arnie?
You're not acting like yourself.

Oh, Mr. Bing–Peezo and I had a HUGE argument yesterday. He thinks I'm an alien doughnut from outer spastry, and I told a hungry lady she should eat him for lunch. But I didn't mean it, Mr. Bing! I just said it because I WAS SO MAD AT HIM!

Well, sometimes even friends argue and say things they don't mean, Arnie. But I'm sure you and Peezo will straighten it out and be laughing about it in no time.

Do you really think so, Mr. Bing? I'm going to call Peezo **RIGHT NOW!**

Mr. Bing is right. I know Peezo doesn't *REALLY* think I'm an alien doughnut. And he must know that I didn't *REALLY* want him to become that hungry lady's lunch.

Hmmm, he's not answering.

He's probably busy at the bowling alley. I know he helps the manager a few days a week polishing bowling balls and spraying deodorant in stinky bowling shoes. I'll just head over there and patch things up with him FACE-TO-FACE. That's probably better anyway.

CHAPTER 5

No one has seen Peezo since yesterday before lunch.

Before

LUNCH.

I wasn't fried yesterday—
I know what that means:

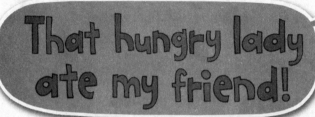

That hungry lady ate my friend!

And to think right now Peezo is sitting all alone, digesting in her **STOMACH.**

IT'S ALL MY FAULT!

OH, PEEZO, CAN YOU EVER FORGIVE ME?!

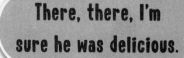

There, there, I'm sure he was delicious.

Excuse me, little doughnut guy— uhhh, I don't want to make things worse, but I think you'd better get over to the Downtown Bakery.

We're here with Mr. Baker Man at the Downtown Bakery, which will be closing its doors **FOR GOOD** next week.

WHAT?! The Downtown Bakery is closing its doors? WHY?!

Ever since the news broke that alien doughnuts are taking over Earth because people eat doughnuts, no one is buying them.

THIS IS THE LAST STRAW!

I'm not going to stand here and let those alien doughnuts . . .

What's happening to me?

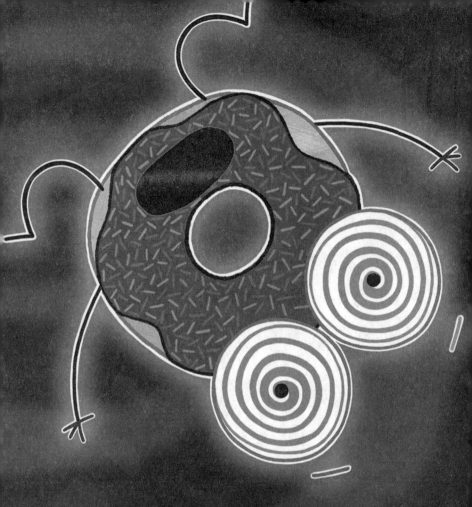

It's as though I'm spinning around in a bubble made of JELLY!

CHAPTER 6

It feels like I went through the Ringy-Dingy Doughnut-Making Thingy® again! Or did someone eat me and I just rolled down into his stomach? Maybe it was that hungry lady who ate Peezo.

WHOA, that lady **was** hungry—there are loads of doughnuts in here! They look so different from any doughnuts I've ever seen before. They're **HUGE!**

Hey, there's a sprinkle
doughnut just like me.
Except she's SQUARE,
her frosting is GREEN,
and her sprinkles are . . .

GLOWING!

Wait a minute.
I know what's going on—

YOU'RE THE ALIEN DOUGHNUTS FROM

OUTER SPASTRY!

I guess Loretta Schmoretta *WAS* telling the truth.

She CANNOT tell a lie.
And neither can I!

LET ME OUT OF
HERE RIGHT NOW!
YOU DON'T SCARE ME—
I'M A DOUGHNUT-DOG!

AND I KNOW
TAE KWON DOUGH!

51

If these alien doughnuts think they can push me around just because I'm little and—

Hey, Earth looks really cool from up here!

I can see the entire town of Yummy Valley! There's the Downtown Bakery and the Fluffy Pup Dog Groomer, where I get fresh frosting and sprinkles, and OH, there's our apartment—

WHAT AM I THINKING?!

I have to FOCUS and figure out a plan to stop these guys from taking over Earth.

I KNOW!

I remember when Mr. Bing tried to eat me I kept yelling at him, but THEN I realized I might make him mad and he'd try to eat me again. SO, I started talking to him in my *sweetest* voice possible so I could trick him and make my escape.

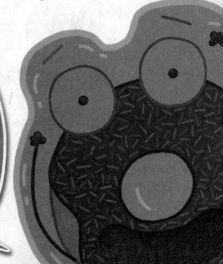

HA!

If it worked on Mr. Bing, I bet it will work on these guys, too.

CHAPTER 7

We must be in a whole other galaxy now because I've never seen planets like THIS before. They actually look like doughnuts! The aliens have the word

UFONUT

programmed into their navigation device. UFONUT must be the name of their planet! I've never heard of it, but apparently it's

12 ZILLION
miles from Earth!

I sure hope this trip counts toward my Frosted Flier Miles.

It looks like we're coming in for a landing. The aliens are arguing about something. I can't understand what they're saying but I can tell they're up to NO GOOD!

HOLEY DOUGHNUTS!

THERE ARE **HUNDREDS** OF THEM! How on EARTH—I mean, how on **UFONUT**— am I going to take them all on by myself?!

I think they just said that they're going to strip me of my sprinkles and frosting, then throw me into a dark and musty DUNGEON with all the other Downtown Bakery doughnuts, then one by one drag us KICKING and SCREAMING into a brightly lit room where they'll try to pump us for information that will help them take over the EARTH.

Well, they won't get a peep out of me!

If only I could find the OTHER Downtown Bakery doughnuts so we could make a plan TOGETHER for how to STOP THESE UFONUTS ONCE AND FOR ALL AND GET BACK HOME.

Actually, I can't decide if we should stop them first and *THEN* get back home **OR** get back home and *THEN* stop them.

Hmmm, WHAT WOULD GEORGE DO?

Stop them first and then get back home. Then brush and floss. Or floss first, THEN brush. I don't know—they didn't make floss in my day. Your call.

Thanks, George! I don't have teeth, but it's good advice.

I have to say, they're not really **acting** like mean alien doughnuts who want to take over Earth. They're being all *POLITE*.

And **FRIENDLY.**

And **MASSAGE-y.**

Could you get the spot right above my top left— **Oh yeah, right there.** Careful of my sprinkles.

But I know that's just what they **WANT** me to think so they can trick me into "spilling the sprinkles," so to speak!

I wonder where they're taking me now.

Look at all these **COOL STORES!**
I think a little window-shopping is just
the thing to clear my mind so I can think
up a good plan. **OOOOH**, these PLANET
UFONUT **T**-shirts **ROCK**. And Mr. Bing
would love a PLANET UFONUT snow globe!
I'll come back and pick one up before I go.
Is THAT a remote-controlled flying cup
and saucer?! Okay, just for the record,
I'm still officially **REALLY MAD**
about all the problems these alien doughnuts have caused, but this place has the

BEST STUFF!

It's the Downtown Bakery doughnuts, and it looks like they're in **TROUBLE!**

CHAPTER 8

CUT! Arnie, is that YOU?

PEEZO!

YOU DIDN'T GET EATEN!

So why did that hungry lady not eat you for lunch?

At the last minute she decided I was too greasy, so she went with a salad instead.

Peezo, I'm sorry I got so mad.

I'm sorry for all the dumb things I said.

Finding out that the hungry lady didn't eat Peezo is the best news I've heard since Mr. Bing told me he wasn't going to eat **ME!** Well, now that Peezo, the Downtown Bakery doughnuts, and I are all here, we can come up with a **SUPER GOOD** plan to stop those **UFONUTS** from taking over Earth.

HEY—

Why did they abduct Peezo, anyway? He's not a doughnut. They must be upset about Earthlings eating *ANYTHING* made of dough. **OH NO**—the situation is even **WORSE** than I **THOUGHT!**

All right, Peezo, I stopped the Ufonuts for the moment, but we have to think fast before they move in again! So here's my idea—

Arnie, the Ufonuts aren't planning on taking over Earth. They're just making a movie.

A movie?

A movie.

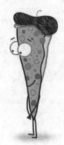

Ooohhh, *I* see. They want you to say that so you don't blow their cover. *GOT* it.

No, they're really making a movie, Arnie. It's called *The Power Pastries and the Rise of the Giant Doughnut Holes.*

Well, if the Ufonuts aren't taking over Earth, then why did they abduct all of us?

Because they're too big to fit in some of the costumes. But Earthling doughnuts are just the right size.

But you're not a doughnut. Do you have a part in the movie, too?

I'm the *DIRECTOR*. That's why they abducted me. They read my movie reviews and thought I'd be perfect for the job. And they abducted you because they want you to play the Caked Crusader, Arnie. Go try on your costume—your big scene is up next!

Oh, poor Peezo!

Those tricky UFONUTS have BRAINWASHED him into thinking he's a BIG-TIME MOVIE DIRECTOR. They've probably brainwashed the Downtown Bakery doughnuts, too. And that means only one thing—**I'M NEXT!** It's all making sense now—the ufonuts are trying to **BRAINWASH** all of us to make us part of their **EVIL PLAN** to take over **EARTH!**

CHAPTER 9

I know I'm on a serious mission and all, but I can't help but notice how **TOTALLY AWESOME** I look. Using my napkin as a cape was my idea. Whatever happens, I can't look the Ufonuts directly in the eyes because that's when the brainwashing starts, I bet. I have to pretend that I'm **ALREADY** brainwashed and that I don't know what they're up to. Off I go—it's **the Caked Crusader** to the rescue!

Ietquut onnut ethut etsut, everyonehut!

Quiet on the set, everyone!

Boy, Peezo sure is convincing as a big-time movie director. They really brainwashed him good. He even speaks **UFONUT!**

Arnie, this is the scene where the Caked Crusader retrieves the Goblet of Golden Glaze from the Bear Claw Cave. All you have to do is sneak up and grab the goblet, replace it with the bag of sprinkles, and run from the Rolling Doughnut Hole. Then as you exit the cave you'll meet up with the tribe of Bear Claws returning home.

GOT IT?

GOT IT.

Oh, I've *GOT IT* all right.

"IT"

being an idea for
the perfect plan!

When I meet up with the tribe of Bear
Claws, I'll surprise them with my expert

TAE KWON DOUGH

moves. They won't know what HIT them!
Then the rest of the Ufonuts will see how

SUPER DANGEROUS

I am and they'll run for cover. Then I'll grab
Peezo and the Downtown Bakery doughnuts
and we'll hop in one of the Ufonuts' flying
cups and saucers and ZIP back to EARTH.
It's the perfect plan! **HA**—this Caked
Crusader thing is going to be a snap!

All right, everyone.
Three, two, and . . .

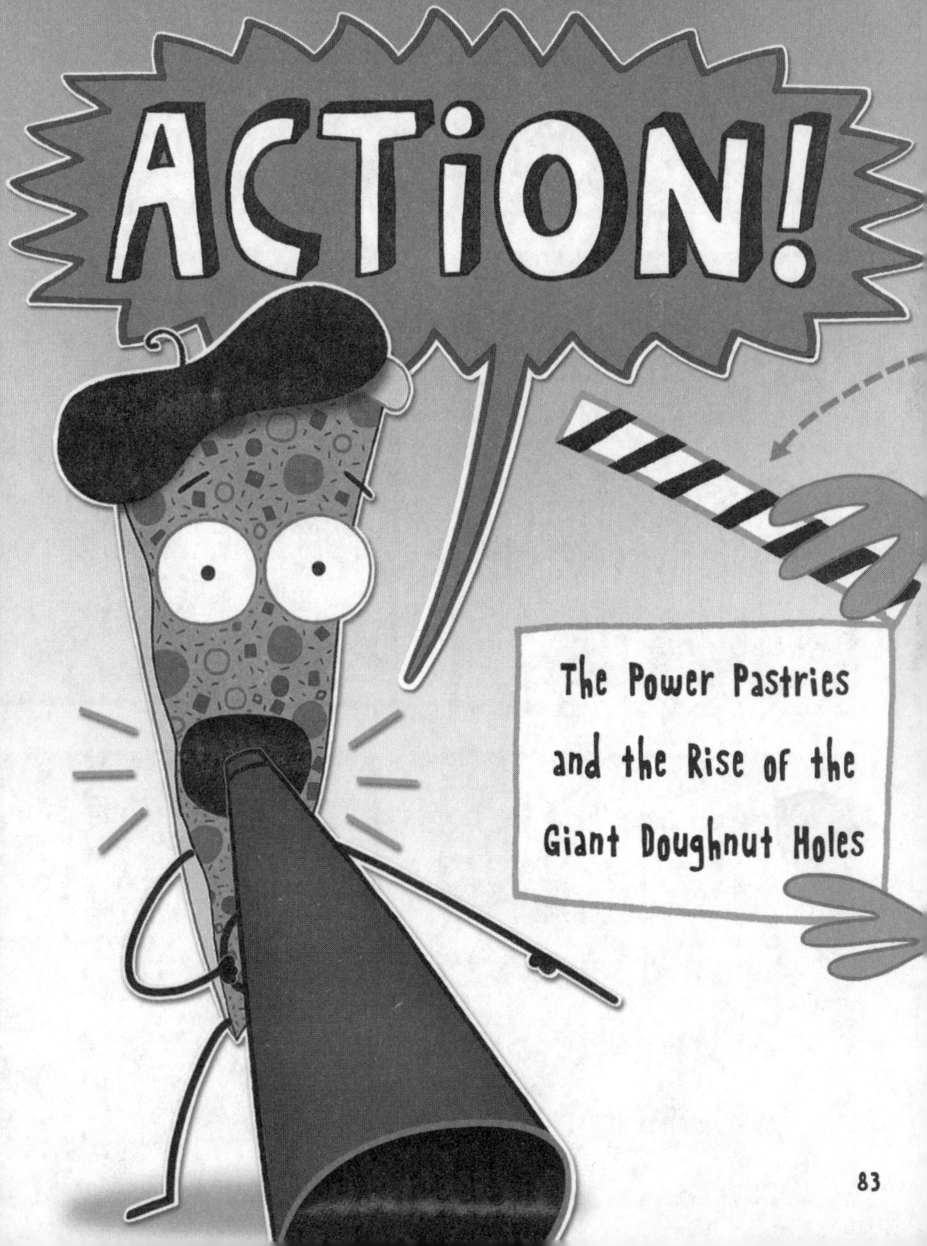

CHAPTER 10

Where am I?

Did I get brainwashed?

Did they finish making the movie?

Is it really impossible to sneeze with your eyes open?

I must have fainted from the shock of seeing those scary alien doughnuts. I guess my perfect plan wasn't so perfect after all.

I hear something happening outside. Are those **EARTHLINGS?** **YES!** There's Mr. Baker Man and Loretta Schmoretta and more Downtown Bakery customers! It looks like Peezo is leading them into a movie theater. **OH NO—** the **UFONUTS** must have tricked them by bringing them here for a movie premiere starring their abducted

doughnuts, but **REALLY** they're about to be brainwashed just like Peezo! I have to get over there before it's **TOO LATE!**

PREMIERE is a French word meaning *FIRST.* By the way, these 3-D glasses look, how you say, *RAD* with my beret, no?

ATTENTION,
EARTHLINGS—
THE MOVIE IS A
FAKE! THE UFONUTS
ARE TRYING TO
BRAINWASH YOU!
DON'T LOOK AT
THE SCREEN!

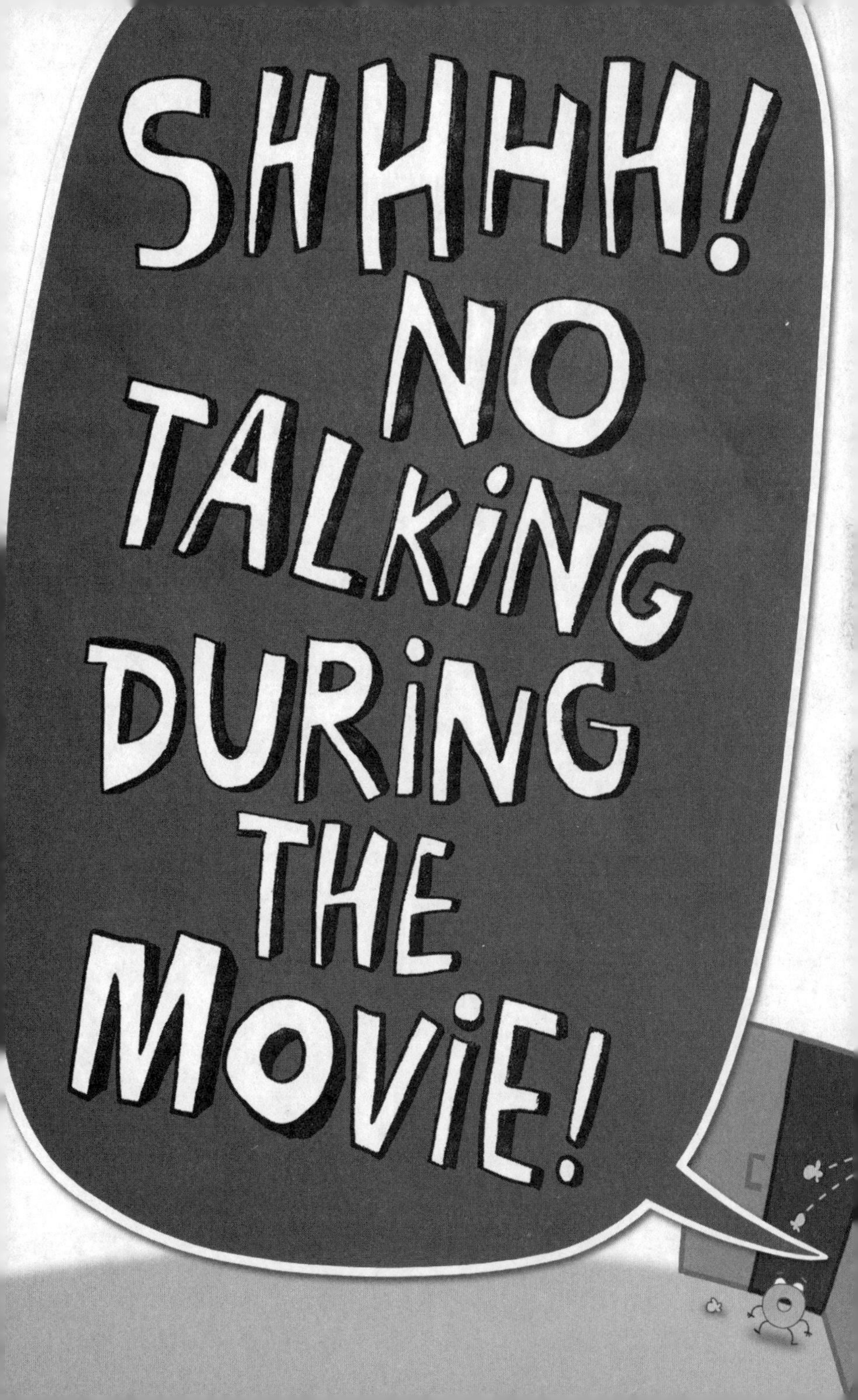
SHHHH! NO TALKING DURING THE MOVIE!

WHAT?!

THEY DON'T BELIEVE ME.

Well, I can't leave them alone in here with these ufonuts. There's no telling **WHAT** will happen to them! I'll have to stay and watch the movie, too, but the second I feel myself getting brainwashed, I'll look away from the screen!

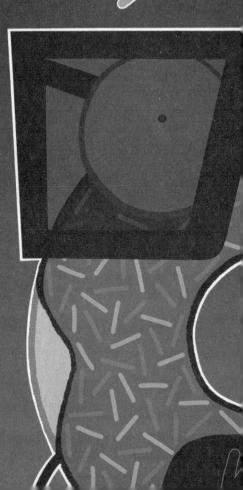

Oooh, here's the scene where I'm being chased by the GIANT ROLLING DOUGHNUT HOLE! It's even scarier in 3-D! I have to admit, if this movie thing weren't a big trick, I'd give it

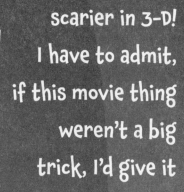

5 out of 5 sprinkles myself. But I can't let that distract me. I MUST STOP THE UFONUTS!

The movie just ended and everyone is busy congratulating Peezo and the Ufonuts, so I ran outside to hide behind the theater. I'm going to watch the Earthlings as they leave to see if they've been brainwashed.

You're such good actors—I couldn't possibly eat you now.

Who knew that I make such talented doughnuts?!

I'm so proud of you!

Well, if you eat us, then we can't be in the sequel!

You were wonderful!

So far there's nothing out of the ordinary. They still seem like regular people having perfectly normal conversations with their doughnuts. Maybe the brainwashing hasn't sunk all the way in yet.

Wait a minute—what's that rumbling sound?

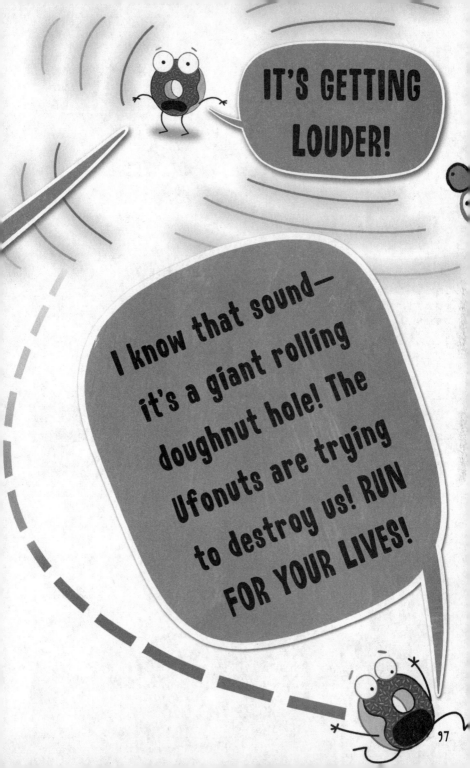

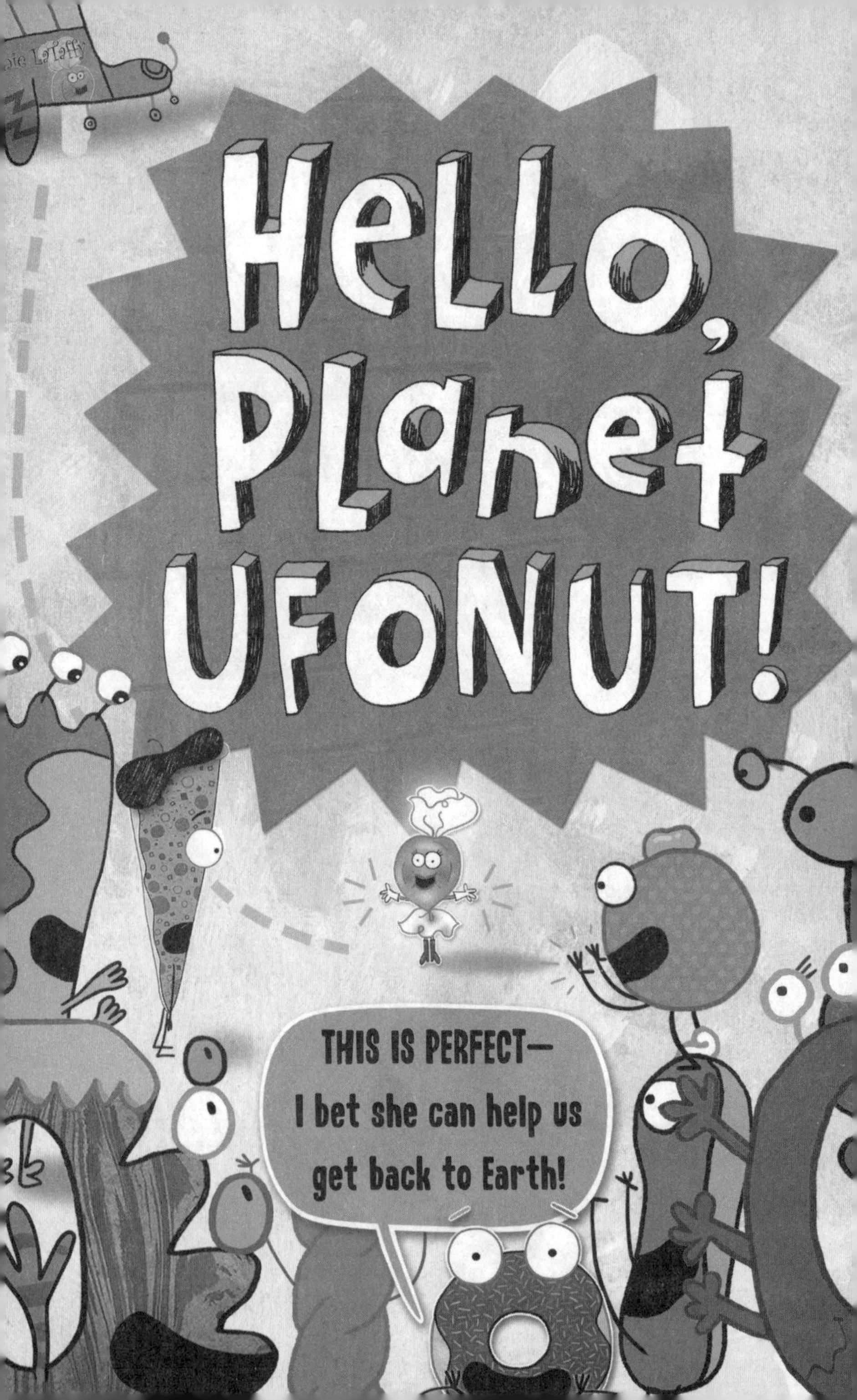
Hello, Planet UFONUT!
THIS IS PERFECT—
I bet she can help us
get back to Earth!

Uh, hi, Queenie LaTaffy. I'm Arnie, your aunt Chewy's next-door neighbor.

Oh, so you must be the doughnut-dog I've heard her talk about!

Right! And this is my friend Peezo. Please excuse him—he's a little nervous because he's your **#1 FAN!** AND he's not quite himself because the Ufonuts brainwashed him and now he thinks he's a **BIG-TIME** movie director.

Thbll Thbllth Bllth Bllthbll

101

Listen, Queenie, I don't want to scare you, but these Ufonuts are planning to take over Earth and . . .

YOU'RE the director?! We got an invitation to the premiere, but we got stuck in space traffic. We made it in time to play at the party, though!

You've heard of the *POWER PASTRIES* movie? So it's— FOR REAL?

It's FOR REAL, all right! The Ufonuts make the best movies in the UNIVERSE!

Well, even if the *MOVIE* is for real, you're not the real *DIRECTOR*, Peezo. It says *DIRECTOR SPIELBERG* on the back of the chair.

I know. That's my last name.

Your full name is *PEEZO SPIELBERG?*

Are you related to . . .

YEAH. We're distant cousins. We don't see each other much, but he's taught me everything he knows about filmmaking.

Director Spielberg

OKAY. So I was wrong about the ufonuts. I'm a big enough doughnut to admit that. But there's one thing I KNOW I'm right about—THEY SURE KNOW HOW TO THROW A PARTY!

Oompah-Oompah WOW-WOW!

Another great thing about the party is that it relaxed Peezo enough to ask Queenie LaTaffy for her autograph. She asked Peezo for *HIS* autograph, too. After all, he's a **BIG-TIME** movie director now. **FOR REAL!**

CHAPTER 11

Well, the movie is "a wrap," as they say in "the BIZ," and the party is over, so it's time for all of us Earthlings to head for home.

Queenie LaTaffy and her band have their own bus, but the ufonuts are giving the rest of us a ride on their **DELUXE** flying cup and saucer limousine.

Now that I've gotten to know the ufonuts, it seems strange that I ever thought they were trying to harm us. I can't believe I'm saying this, but I think I'm actually going to

MiSS THEM!

I'm sure we'll stay in touch, though. Peezo said they're already talking about making a

sequel! I'm going to ask him if I could be his assistant director. One thing is for sure—my days of running from giant rolling doughnut holes are

O-V-E-R!

For now, I'm just ready to get home and see Mr. Bing. He's probably worried SICK wondering where I am.

I never meant to be gone for so long, but I was abducted by those alien doughnuts, Mr. Bing! They're called **UFONUTS** and it turns out they weren't trying to take over Earth. They were just making a movie, and I played the **Caked Crusader!** I tried to call you to let you know where I was, but I couldn't get a signal from up there.

TRY **PHONEY BALONEY!** UNLIMITED MINUTES and GUARANTEED service to ANY planet within 20 ZILLION miles of EARTH!

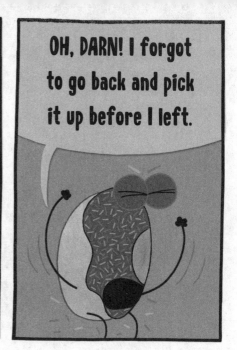

I'm not being silly, Mr. Bing—I really was there! Oh, wait, I can prove it. I brought you a Planet Ufonut SNOW GLOBE.

OH, DARN! I forgot to go back and pick it up before I left.

Planet Ufonut. Good one, Arnie. Sounds like something Loretta Schmoretta would think up!

CHAPTER 12

Now that people know
the Ufonuts aren't going
to take over Earth, Mr. Baker
Man was able to open the doors
of the Downtown Bakery again. In fact,
a lot of people are actually *HOPING* the
Ufonuts will come back after they heard
about the movie. I guess **EVERYONE**
wants to be a STAR.

I've been told I have the
face for the silver screen!
Or maybe that was radio.
WHATEVER—I'm ready!

Peezo is still on **CLOUD NINE** after meeting Queenie LaTaffy. She told Peezo the next time she visits her aunt Chewy she'd let him know. As for me, I'm trying out a little something I learned from Peezo while we filmed the movie. I thought it was impressive how when he said,

CUT!

everyone stopped what they were doing, and when he said,

ACTION!

they started moving again. I think I could really get some use out of that, too. Oooh, Mr. Bing is taking out the garbage. This is the perfect chance to give it a try!

You scared me! What did you say?

I said, "CUT!" That means you're supposed to stop and listen for direction.

I don't need direction. I'm just taking out the garbage.

Right, but I think you can do it with a little more drama, Mr. Bing. Now try it again, but THIS time walk across the parking lot more quickly and look back and forth a few times, like you think someone is following you. Like THIS.

I'm not going to do that, Arnie.

GARBAGE

And
ACTION!

Good . . . good. **CUT!**
You stumbled a little that
time, so try it again.

Mr. Bing, I said, **"CUT!"**
You have to stop and listen
to me, remember?

119

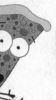

HOW TO SPEAK UFONUT

Speaking UFONUT is a lot like speaking PIG LATIN, only instead of words ending in AY or WAY, they end in UT or NUT.

If a word starts with a CONSONANT or a group of consonants, just move it/them to the end of the word. Then add UT. Let's try it with the words PIE and CRUST.

Move the "P" from the front of the word to the back.

Add "UT" at the end.

PIE → IEP → IEPUT

Move the "CR" from the front of the word to the back.

Add "UT" at the end.

CRUST → USTCR → USTCRUT

If a word starts with a vowel—**a**, **e**, **i**, **o**, and **u**—like **EYE**, **OWN**, and **UNDER**, just add **NUT** at the end.

OWNNUT

EYENUT

UNDERNUT

ARNIENUT!

EXACTLYNUT!

Sometimes **y** is used as a vowel, like in **MY**, **CRY**, and **FLY**. **WHY?**

Right!

In that case, move the consonants that come before the **y** to the end of the word and add **UT**. That's all there is to it!

TRY TO FIGURE THIS OUT:

Inut onderwut atwhut Arnie'snut extnut adventurenut illwut ebut!

Hmmmmmm.

I KNOW! You said, "I wonder what Arnie's next adventure will be!"

That's it!

Oh yeah!

ARNIE'S NEXT ADVENTURE:

When Arnie and his pals compete in their favorite TV reality show, they face some unexpected twists and turns in the race to the finish line.

WOOHOO! I can hardly wait!

I hope you'll be there to cheer us on!

To Rilynne—

my favorite little Earthlingnut

SQUARE
FISH

An Imprint of Macmillan
175 Fifth Avenue
New York, NY 10010
mackids.com

Square Fish and the Square Fish logo are trademarks of Macmillan and are used by
Henry Holt and Company, LLC under license from Macmillan.

Our books may be purchased in bulk for promotional, educational, or business use. Please contact your
local bookseller or the Macmillan Corporate and Premium Sales Department at (800) 221-7945
ext. 5442 or by e-mail at MacmillanSpecialMarkets@macmillan.com.

Library of Congress Cataloging-in-Publication Data
Keller, Laurie.
Invasion of the Ufonuts / Laurie Keller.
pages   cm. — (The adventures of Arnie the doughnut ; [2])
"Christy Ottaviano Books."
Summary: "Arnie is shocked when he hears his neighbor Loretta Schmoretta tell news reporters that she
was the victim of an alien abduction. And not just any aliens—alien doughnuts from outer spastry. Arnie
thinks this is a crazy story, that is, until he gets abducted. Arnie must think fast in order to rescue
his fellow doughnuts and the townspeople from the alien invaders" —Provided by publisher.
ISBN 978-1-250-07965-7 (paperback)
[1. Doughnuts—Fiction. 2. Alien abduction—Fiction. 3. Humorous stories.] I. Title.
PZ7.K281346In 2014   [Fic]—dc23   2013042139

Originally published in the United States by Christy Ottaviano Books/Henry Holt and Company, LLC
First Square Fish Edition: 2016
Square Fish logo designed by Filomena Tuosto

9 10 8

AR: 1.0 / LEXILE: 730L

GOFISH

LAURIE KELLER

What did you want to be when you grew up?
I remember wanting to be a TV weather person. I was fascinated with weather and liked watching David Compton report the weather on the local Channel 13 news!

When did you realize you wanted to be an illustrator?
Not until I was out of high school. I always loved art and took every art class available all through school, but I didn't realize I could do it as a job until I went with a friend to a student art exhibit at Kendall College of Art and Design. I enrolled there the following fall and got my degree in illustration. I worked for seven years as a greeting card artist for Hallmark before getting into children's books.

What's your most embarrassing childhood memory?
My skirt got stuck in a folding chair in choir practice, and when we were all supposed to stand and sing, I couldn't get up. The choir director was a very *gruff* sort, and when he saw me sitting, he pounded on the piano, stopped everyone from singing, and asked what I was doing. It was quite humiliating to explain. My face is turning red all over again just thinking about it!

As a young person, who did you look up to most?
My mom.

Where do you work on your illustrations?
In my studio. Sometimes in the early sketch stages I sit outside, but most of the art is done inside at my desk.

Where do you find inspiration for your illustrations?
I have a huge collection of books that I like to thumb through, but lately I've been looking on Pinterest. I'm addicted!

What sparked your imagination for *Invasion of the Ufonuts*?
I'm an avid doodler—especially while talking on the phone—and one day I was scribbling some odd shapes with eyes and mouths and some of them looked like alien doughnuts. VOILÀ! My next Arnie idea was born!

Have you ever seen any suspicious signs of alien doughnuts on Earth?
Wait a minute. Maybe it *wasn't* me who thought of the idea for *Invasion of the Ufonuts*. Maybe alien doughnuts took over my brain and *MADE* me draw doodles that looked like them so I would tell their story! Hmmm, very suspicious, INDEED!

What can readers look forward to in Arnie's next adventure, *The Spinny Icky Showdown*?
No spoilers, please!
Arnie and Peezo compete on their favorite TV game show when it comes to town and face some unexpected challenges (and Peezo's worst fear—Nick Pumpernickel!) when the games begin!

What is your favorite thing about Arnie?
He's very adventurous and wants to get the most out of life.

What is your favorite kind of doughnut?
I've literally NEVER had a doughnut I don't like, but my favorite is the Krispy Kreme vanilla-filled, chocolate-covered doughnut. It kind of covers all the bases. I keep hearing how delicious Cronuts are, and I'm eager to try one! MMMMM . . . doughnuts (don't tell Arnie).

Where do you go for peace and quiet?
A walk by Lake Michigan or in the woods.

Who is your favorite fictional character?
If I had to pick just one, I'd choose Charlie Brown. He's so contemplative and kindhearted, and I love his tenacity despite living in a world that often disappoints him.

If you could travel in time, where would you go and what would you do?
I would zip back to the early 1500s and see if I could be Michelangelo's gofer as he painted the Sistine Chapel, for starters. I'm fascinated with that time period, but to see him paint would be amazing.

What do you want readers to remember about your books?
Hopefully, that they had a laugh or two while reading them. One of my favorite things is when people tell me what lines in my books made them laugh. It doesn't get much better than that!

What would you do if you ever stopped illustrating?

If I were ever good enough, I'd love to be a banjo player in a bluegrass band. I've tinkered with the banjo on and off for years—mostly off, until recently. I take lessons again and make time each day to practice. I also get together with some talented musician friends to play music. It makes me 100 percent happy!

Do you have any strange or funny habits? Did you when you were a kid?

If there are two items left on the shelf at a grocery store and I only need one, I have to buy both because it makes me feel too sad leaving the one by itself. I've been that way ever since I was little. I figured I'd grow out of it, but I think it's actually gotten worse!

As a kid, I didn't like uneven numbers. So when I would run scared up the stairs from the basement, I would step on the third step twice so it would make an even number of steps.

What do you wish you could do better?

Public speaking. I've always been terrified of it and used to avoid it at all costs. It's gotten easier for me over the years, but I'm by no means a natural at it. One thing that has helped is to set really low standards for myself: if I don't cry, faint, or vomit during a presentation, then I've hit it out of the park! I really admire people who can get up in front of a large group and speak to them as though it's a room full of their best friends.

What would your readers be most surprised to learn about you?

How long it takes me to write my books. Once in a while they come together in a timely manner, but I second-guess myself again and again and again (and again and again), so it really slows down the process. I would love to be able to change that!

Who is your favorite artist?
If I had to pick one, I'd choose Delphine Durand.

What is your favorite medium to work in?
Acrylic paint and collage.

What was your favorite book or comic/graphic novel when you were a kid? What's your current favorite?
Nancy was my most favorite comic book as a kid, followed by *Richie Rich* and *Little Lulu*. These are probably hybrid graphic novel/chapter books, but I really like *Diary of a Wimpy Kid, Captain Underpants*, and *Dear Dumb Diary*. Janet Tashjian's My Life books are very entertaining. The Just Grace books by Charise Mericle Harper have elements of a graphic novel in them, and I think they're spectacular.

What challenges do you face in the artistic process, and how do you overcome them?
I can easily make my illustrations too busy and cluttered. Sometimes it works okay, but many times I have to go back in and simplify them.

If you could travel anywhere in the world, where would you go and what would you do?
I've traveled quite a bit around the world, but the place I most want to go is Alaska. I'd camp and hike and soak up the great outdoors there. Maybe have tea with a grizzly bear?!

Arnie steps up to the plate in a sensational game show competition!

Let the games begin!
Read on for a sneak peek.

WE CAN'T RIGHT NOW! We have to keep our fingers crossed for good luck until *The SPINNY ICKY SHOWDOWN* comes back from commercial!

Well, no fancy new thingamajig for you, then, but GOOD LUCK!

DARN, I would have liked a fancy new thing-amajig, but we CAN'T uncross our fingers because RICKy MaverICK, the host of The SPINNY ICKy SHOWDOWN, is about to announce the **one** and **only** town they're going to travel to for their season finale! The SPINNY ICKy SHOWDOWN is the BEST show on TV, and Peezo and I want to compete on it more than anything. Even Mr. Bing likes to watch it, which is saying a lot because he doesn't like the shows

DING DONG DOOFUS,
NOGGIN KNOCKERS,
OR
PLEASE STOP
SNEEZING ON ME!

Peezo comes over every Friday night to watch *The SPINNY ICKy SHOWDOWN* with us. We laugh really hard through the whole show because the *ICKSTERS* (the contestants) have to do all sorts of crazy

iCK-related things like painting a piCKet fence with lipstiCK or jumping like criCKets over candlestiCKs.

The *ICKSTERS* compete in teams of two and one team gets eliminated after each round. At the end of the competition both members of the winning *ICKS* team are presented with a **BIG, SHINY ICKS TROPHY** with their **VERY OWN NAME** engraved on it!

YOUR NAME HERE

When Peezo and I heard that *The SPINNY ICKy SHOWDOWN* was taking their show on the road, we sent in our entry forms **RIGHT AWAY** hoping they'd pick *YUMMY VALLEY* and choose us to be an *ICKSTER* team! We had to make up a team name so we chose

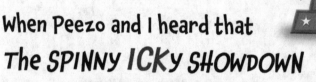

The **DOUGH BROS**

since we're both made of dough and we're **SUCH GOOD FRIENDS** we're almost like brothers, or **BROS** for short.

We're back, everyone, and it's the moment you've all been waiting for. We're ready to announce the one and only town we'll visit for the season finale of The SPINNY ICKY SHOWDOWN! DRUM ROLL, PLEASE.
Eh-hem, I said, DRUM ROLL PLEASE!
That's ODD. Drum Roll Guy is ALWAYS right here whenever I call for a drum roll.
Does anyone know where he is?